The 50 United States

Written by Karen Price and Raymond Miller
Designed by Dan Jankowski

References
Ambrose, Stephen. *Undaunted Courage*. New York:
Simon & Schuster, 1996.
U.S. Census Bureau, 1990 census results released 1996.
The World Book Multimedia Encyclopedia,
copyright 1995 by World Book, Inc.

© 2000 by Pace Products, Inc.
Published by Tangerine Press™, an imprint of Scholastic Inc.
555 Broadway, New York, NY 10012

Tangerine Press™ and associated logo and design are trademarks of Scholastic Inc.
Printed in Canada
ISBN 0-439-25391-8
10 9 8 7 6 5 4 3 2 1

P9-AGU-401

Celebrating the 50 States!

If you open an American history book, you can find out about everything from the Revolutionary War to the Apollo moon missions. Flip through a United States geography book and you'll see amazing pictures of the Grand Canyon and the Statue of Liberty. Now, there's another way to explore the rich history, tradition, and geography of the United States. Just pick up a quarter and look at the "tails" side!

On December 1, 1997, President Clinton signed the "50 State Quarters™ Program Act." This act allows the Department of the Treasury to issue a series of new quarters honoring the 50 states. From 1999 to 2008, five state quarters will be issued each year in the order the states became part of the United States of America.

Starting with Delaware and ending with Hawaii, each special-edition quarter will feature a design unique to its state. You never know what design will be on your quarters. You might find George Washington crossing the Delaware River, or Connecticut's majestic Charter Oak tree. The 50 State Quarter Program will definitely have you taking a closer look at your change.

Starting a 50 State Quarters Collection

These quarters make an impressive addition to any coin collection. For people who don't already have a coin collection, these quarters are the perfect starting point!

You can keep your quarters in a variety of collector's coin folders. To add a quarter to your collection, put the quarter in the circular slot and press. The quarter will stay in place.

"Changing" History

Although the 50 State Quarters Program will change the appearance of the quarter, it isn't the first time the coin has received a new look. From the late 18th century to the early 20th century, the quarter featured the same two symbols. The front pictured Lady Liberty, but her position, hair, and dress have changed from time to time. The back pictured our national bird, the bald eagle. It, too, changed in appearance over time. The eagle started out as a small bird, which many people thought looked like a pigeon. Eventually, the eagle design was changed to reflect a strong and proud image.

**Front of 1804
Lady Liberty Quarter**

To celebrate the *bicentennial* (200-year anniversary) of George Washington's birthday, in 1932 a silhouette of Washington's head replaced Lady Liberty on the front of the quarter. It has appeared there ever since. In 1976, the United States celebrated the bicentennial of the signing of the Declaration of Independence. That event marked a temporary change in the quarter's appearance. In 1975 and 1976, a colonial drummer replaced the eagle. From 1977 to 1999, the quarter's design remained the same.

**Back of 1975–1976
Bicentennial Quarter**

Another Change

With the 50 State Quarters Program, the quarter will go through the biggest design changes in history. The eagle emblem on the back of the quarter will be replaced with designs representing each state. To make as much room as possible, the words "United States of America" and "Quarter Dollar" are being moved from the back of the coin to the front. Look at the illustrations below to compare the old and new designs.

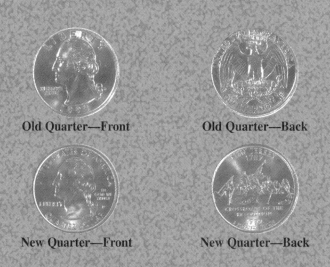

Old Quarter—Front   Old Quarter—Back

New Quarter—Front   New Quarter—Back

Design Your State's Quarter!

The best part about the 50 State Quarters Program is that anyone can submit a design for approval. That means you can try designing the back of your state's quarter.* Use the guide on the opposite page to draw your own design. If you don't want to ruin the page by cutting it, trace the guide on blank paper.

*Some of the state quarters designs have already been selected. To find out if your state's quarter has been designed, contact your governor's office or log on to the United States Mint website at *www.usmint.gov/50states*. You can find out much more about the 50 State Quarters Program there.

Before you begin your design, read these important guidelines.

- Designs may include state landmarks (natural and man-made), landscapes, historic buildings, symbols of state resources or industries, official flowers and trees, state images (such as a cactus for Arizona or a bronco for Wyoming), and state outlines.
- Your design should appeal to all citizens of the state. Do not include subjects or symbols that may offend anyone.
- Do not use state flags, state seals, and words or phrases in your design.
- Do not include a head-and-shoulders portrait of any person, living or dead, or any portrait of a living person in your design.

You must submit your design idea to your state governor's office. The governor will select at least three and no more than five designs. The governor will then send the designs to the United States Mint. There, the approved design concepts will be drawn by artists and returned to the governor, who will choose one of those designs.

Leave this area blank.

Leave this area blank.

Alabama
"The Heart of Dixie"

Capital	**State Bird**
Montgomery	Yellowhammer
State Flower	**Land Area**
Camellia	50,750 sq. mi.
	(131,443 sq. km)
State Tree	**Rank in Size**
Southern pine	28th

In 1682, French explorer LaSalle sailed to the mouth of the Mississippi River, then claimed for France all the land drained by the Mississippi, including present-day **Alabama**. In 1702, two French-Canadian brothers founded Fort Louis along the Mobile River. Flooding in 1711 forced them to move the settlement south to present-day Mobile. Fort Louis was renamed Fort Conde in 1720 and was made the capital of French Louisiana.

France gave almost all its U.S. land to Great Britain in 1763. In 1783, Great Britain turned most of Alabama over to Spain. In 1795, the United States and Spain signed the Treaty of San Lorenzo, which gave the area, including present-day Alabama, to the United States. It was then called the Mississippi Territory. In 1817, the area became known as the Alabama Territory. It became the 22nd state in 1819.

 Statehood Year: 1819
The 22nd state
Coin Issue Year: 2003

Alaska
"The Last Frontier"

Capital	**State Bird**
Juneau	Willow ptarmigan
State Flower	**Land Area**
Forget-me-not	570,374 sq. mi.
	(1,477,268 sq. km)
State Tree	**Rank in Size**
Sitka spruce	1st

The United States bought **Alaska** from Russia in 1867. At first, many Americans thought the purchase was foolish. But Alaska had many natural resources that proved valuable, such as timber, fish, minerals, and oil. In 1880 and again in 1896, gold was discovered in Alaska. This discovery brought thousands of people to the state.

In 1942, the Japanese occupied two Alaskan islands during World War II. That same year the United States government built a military supply road to Alaska, called the Alaska Highway. This highway allowed people to move more freely from the lower 48 states to Alaska. After the war, many Americans agreed that Alaska should be given statehood. This was finally accomplished in 1959.

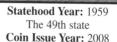 **Statehood Year:** 1959
The 49th state
Coin Issue Year: 2008

Arizona
"The Grand Canyon State"

Capital Phoenix	**State Bird** Cactus wren
State Flower Saguaro (giant cactus)	**Land Area** 113,642 sq. mi. (294,333 sq. km)
State Tree Paloverde	**Rank in Size** 6th

In the 1600s, missionaries from the Roman Catholic church set up missions in the region of **Arizona**. Spaniards founded Arizona's first European settlement at Tubac in 1752. When the Mexican-American War ended in 1848, the United States gained possession of Arizona. In the late 1800s, many people came to Arizona to mine its gold, silver, and copper deposits, settling boom towns such as Tombstone.

In 1890, many in the state voiced their desire for statehood. But the United States government's disagreement with some articles in the state's constitution held things up, and Arizona did not become a state until 1912.

 Statehood Year: 1912 The 48th state **Coin Issue Year:** 2008

Arkansas
"The Land of Opportunity"

Capital Little Rock	**State Bird** Mockingbird
State Flower Apple blossom	**Land Area** 52,075 sq. mi. (134,875 sq. km)
State Tree Pine tree	**Rank in Size** 27th

In 1686, French explorer Henri de Tonti established **Arkansas** Post, the first European settlement in the Arkansas region. Arkansas was part of the U.S. purchase of Louisiana from France in 1803. In 1812, Arkansas was included in the Missouri Territory. To protect settlers against Indians, the U.S. government built Fort Smith in 1817. In 1819, the U.S. government changed the area's name to the Arkansaw Territory.

When Arkansas became a state in 1836, the issue of slavery was being debated in the South. In 1861, after the start of the Civil War, Arkansas seceded (withdrew) from the Union to support the Confederacy (the states that wanted to keep slavery). In 1868, Arkansas was readmitted into the Union.

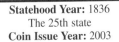 **Statehood Year:** 1836 The 25th state **Coin Issue Year:** 2003

California
"The Golden State"

Capital	**State Bird**
Sacramento	California valley quail
State Flower	**Land Area**
Golden poppy	155,973 sq. mi.
	(403,971 sq. km)
State Tree	
California redwood	**Rank in Size**
	3rd

In 1769, the Spanish governor of Baja **California** and a Franciscan missionary established a mission and a fort, or presidio, at present-day San Diego. Between 1769 and 1823, the Franciscans built 20 more missions, where the natives were taught Christianity.

California became a province of Mexico in 1822, right after Mexico won independence from Spain. In 1841, settlers from the East formed wagon trains and crossed the country to settle in California. These settlers wanted California to become part of the United States, but Mexico did not want to sell its territory. After a two-year war, Mexico surrendered to California in 1848. California became a state in 1850, just two years after gold was discovered there and thousands of people flocked to the state to make their fortunes.

 Statehood Year: 1850
The 31st state
Coin Issue Year: 2005

Colorado
"The Centennial State"

Capital	**State Bird**
Denver	Lark bunting
State Flower	**Land Area**
Rocky Mountain	103,729 sq. mi.
columbine	(268,658 sq. km)
State Tree	**Rank in Size**
Colorado blue spruce	8th

Spain gave the **Colorado** region to Mexico in 1821. In 1833, the first permanent American settlement, Bent's Fort, was established there. After the Mexican-American War ended in 1848, the United States took over the western region of present-day Colorado.

Gold was discovered in Colorado in 1858, and nearly 100,000 people rushed to the region. Those who stayed called the area the Jefferson Territory. The U.S. Congress refused to recognize this territory, and in 1861 set up the Colorado Territory, which had the same boundaries as the present-day state. During Colorado's early days, troops battled Cheyenne, Arapaho, and Ute Indians. In 1870, the railroad joined Colorado to the East, and more people came to the territory. In 1876, Colorado achieved statehood.

Statehood Year: 1876
The 38th state
Coin Issue Year: 2006

Connecticut
"The Constitution State"

Capital	**State Bird**
Hartford	American robin
State Flower	**Land Area**
Mountain laurel	4,845 sq. mi.
	(12,550 sq. km)
State Tree	
White oak	**Rank in Size**
	48th

Connecticut was settled by English colonists from Massachusetts in 1633. In 1636, the settlements of Windsor, Hartford, and Wethersfield came together to form the Connecticut Colony. The king of England gave the Connecticut Colony a charter (similar to a contract) in 1662 granting them a strip of land bordered by a Connecticut bay on one side and the Pacific Ocean on the other. Neither the king nor the colonists realized that the Pacific Ocean was thousands of miles away!

In 1665, the Connecticut Colony became larger when it joined the New Haven Colony. The colony supported independence from Great Britain and sent hundreds of men to fight in the Revolutionary War. Connecticut became one of the original 13 United States in 1788.

 Statehood Year: 1788
The 5th state
Coin Issue Year: 1999

Delaware
"The First State"

Capital	**State Bird**
Dover	Blue hen chicken
State Flower	**Land Area**
Peach blossom	1,955 sq. mi.
	(5,063 sq. km)
State Tree	
American holly	**Rank in Size**
	49th

Delaware was first settled in 1631 by the Dutch, who called the region Zwaanendael. But by 1632, all the settlers had been killed by Indians. In 1638, Peter Minuit, who was responsible for purchasing the island of Manhattan from the Indians, was hired by Sweden to lead a group of Swedish settlers to the region. They called the colony New Sweden.

In 1664, the British took over. They gave the land to William Penn to add to his colony of Pennsylvania. But by 1701, the area became a separate region called the Three Lower Colonies. It was not called Delaware until 1776, after Lord De La Warr, the first governor of the Virginia colony. Delaware was the first state to approve the United States Constitution, and became a state in 1787.

 Statehood Year: 1787
The 1st state
Coin Issue Year: 1999

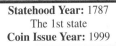

Florida
"The Sunshine State"

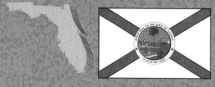

Capital Tallahassee	**State Bird** Mockingbird
State Flower Orange blossom	**Land Area** 53,997 sq. mi. (139,853 sq. km)
State Tree Sabal palm	**Rank in Size** 26th

In 1513, Spanish explorer Juan Ponce de León arrived in **Florida**. He thought Florida was an island and claimed it for Spain. The king of Spain ordered him to colonize the land. When he tried to do so in 1521, he and his men were attacked by Indians, and Ponce de León was wounded by an arrow. With other survivors, he sailed to Cuba, where he died.

The French came to settle in 1564, but were driven out by the Spaniards in 1565. That same year the Spaniards settled St. Augustine, the first permanent European settlement in the United States. For most of the next 200 years, Spain ruled the Florida region. In 1819, Spain gave Florida to the United States. Florida was admitted to the Union in 1845.

Statehood Year: 1845
The 27th state
Coin Issue Year: 2004

Georgia
"The Empire State of the South"

Capital Atlanta	**State Bird** Brown thrasher
State Flower Cherokee rose	**Land Area** 57,919 sq. mi. (150,010 sq. km)
State Tree Live oak	**Rank in Size** 21st

In the 1500s, the Spaniards claimed the southeastern United States, including Florida and **Georgia**. But in 1564, the French set up a colony in Florida. Spain fought and defeated France for control of the land. Then, ignoring the claims of Spain, the British settled near Savannah in 1733. They fought Spain over the Florida-Georgia boundary in 1739. The British lost that battle, but fought the Spaniards again in 1742 and won control of Georgia.

In 1754, Georgia became a royal province, governed by England's King George. When the American Revolution broke out, most Georgians fought for independence. After the war, Georgia approved the United States Constitution and in 1788 became the fourth state admitted to the Union.

Statehood Year: 1788
The 4th state
Coin Issue Year: 1999

Hawaii
"The Aloha State"

Capital	**State Bird**
Honolulu	Hawaiian goose
State Flower	**Land Area**
Yellow hibiscus	6,423 sq. mi.
	(16,637 sq. km)
State Tree	
Kukui	**Rank in Size**
	47th

The Hawaiian Islands were unknown to most of the world until British Captain James Cook stopped there in 1778. He named the islands the Sandwich Islands. For many years, **Hawaii** was a monarchy (governed by a king or queen). But in 1893, a revolution removed the queen from office. In 1900, Hawaii was made a United States territory. Soon after, the U.S. Navy built a base in Pearl Harbor. That base was involved in a major event in United States history. On December 7, 1941, 33 Japanese ships and about 360 airplanes attacked Pearl Harbor. About 3,700 people lost their lives. This event pulled the United States into World War II. During the war many Hawaiian citizens proved their loyalty to the United States, and in 1959 Hawaii became a state.

 Statehood Year: 1959
The 50th state
Coin Issue Year: 2008

Idaho
"The Gem State"

Capital	**State Bird**
Boise	Mountain bluebird
State Flower	**Land Area**
Syringa	82,751 sq. mi.
	(214,325 sq. km)
State Tree	
Western	**Rank in Size**
white pine	11th

Explorers Lewis and Clark traveled through **Idaho** in 1805. Their expedition enabled the U.S. government to claim the Oregon region, which included the present-day states of Oregon, Washington, and Idaho. In 1809, a British fur trader moved into the area. He was soon followed by other traders. In 1860, a group of Mormons (a religious group) settled the first permanent town in Idaho, called Franklin. Soon gold was discovered in Orofino Creek, and people rushed to the region.

In 1863, the Idaho Territory was organized. Silver and lead mines were discovered in northern Idaho in the late 1800s. The mines and the development of the railroad brought more settlers. In 1890, Idaho became the 43rd state.

 Statehood Year: 1890
The 43rd state
Coin Issue Year: 2007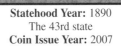

Illinois
"The Land of Lincoln"

Indiana
"The Hoosier State"

Capital Springfield	**State Bird** Cardinal	**Capital** Indianapolis	**State Bird** Cardinal
State Flower Native violet	**Land Area** 55,593 sq. mi. (143,987 sq. km)	**State Flower** Peony	**Land Area** 35,870 sq. mi. (92,904 sq. km)
State Tree White oak	**Rank in Size** 24th	**State Tree** Tulip tree	**Rank in Size** 38th

French explorers Marquette and Jolliet are thought to be the first Europeans to travel through **Illinois**. Later, in 1699, French priests founded a mission in a fur-trading post. The first permanent European settlement, Cahokia, was established in 1699, and another settlement, Kaskaskia, was founded in 1703.

In 1717, Illinois became part of Louisiana, which was a French colony at the time. In 1763, after Great Britain's victory in the French and Indian War, the British owned the colony. After the Revolutionary War, Illinois became part of the Northwest Territory. In 1800, it became part of the Indiana Territory, and in 1809 it was called the Illinois Territory and was made up of present-day Illinois and Wisconsin. In 1818, Illinois became a state.

Fur traders from France, then Great Britain, were the first Europeans to settle in **Indiana**. The French built Indiana's first settlement and fort, called Vincennes, in about 1732. After the French were defeated in 1763, the British took over the fur trade in Indiana and surrounding areas.

Indiana became part of the Northwest Territory after the Revolutionary War. In 1800, Congress established the Indiana Territory, which included the present-day states of Indiana, Illinois, Wisconsin, and parts of Michigan and Minnesota. At first, the territory had to contend with Indian forces, led by Tecumseh. But the Indians were defeated in 1811. In 1816, Indiana became the 19th state to join the Union.

Statehood Year: 1818
The 21st state
Coin Issue Year: 2003

Statehood Year: 1816
The 19th state
Coin Issue Year: 2002

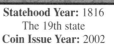

Iowa
"The Hawkeye State"

Capital Des Moines	**State Bird** Eastern goldfinch
State Flower Wild rose	**Land Area** 55,875 sq. mi. (144,716 sq. km)
State Tree Oak	**Rank in Size** 23rd

In 1808, the U.S. Army built **Iowa**'s first fort, Fort Madison. Four years later, the U.S. government acknowledged the Iowa region as part of the Missouri Territory. Outside settlers couldn't move there because the government held the land for Indians. In 1831, the United States government wanted the Native Americans who lived in Illinois to move to Iowa. Chief Black Hawk refused to move. This led to the Black Hawk War of 1832. After the Native American tribes were defeated, they gave up a strip of land along the Mississippi River. Settlers quickly moved into this land, establishing the first permanent settlements in Iowa. In 1838, the United States government created the Territory of Iowa. In 1846, Iowa became a state.

 Statehood Year: 1846
The 29th state
Coin Issue Year: 2004

Kansas
"The Sunflower State"

Capital Topeka	**State Bird** Western meadowlark
State Flower Sunflower	**Land Area** 81,823 sq. mi. (211,922 sq. km)
State Tree Cottonwood	**Rank in Size** 13th

Kansas was part of the land France sold to the United States in the 1803 Louisiana Purchase. When the Santa Fe Trail opened in 1821, many travelers passed through Kansas on their way west. The Kansas town of Council Grove was a main stopping point in the trail. Fort Leavenworth was established in 1827 as the first U.S Army outpost in the area.

In 1825, the U.S. government gave the Indians land in Kansas in return for taking land from them in the East. About 30 Indian tribes settled in the region of Kansas. By 1850, more and more European settlers wanted to live there, so the government took back much of the Indians' land. The Indians fought back, but eventually most of them were moved to Oklahoma. In 1854, Congress established the Territory of Kansas, and in 1861, Kansas became a state.

 Statehood Year: 1861
The 34th state
Coin Issue Year: 2005

Kentucky
"The Bluegrass State"

Capital	State Bird
Frankfort	Kentucky cardinal

State Flower	Land Area
Goldenrod	39,732 sq. mi.
	(102,907 sq. km)

State Tree	Rank in Size
Kentucky coffeetree	36th

In 1774, a group from Pennsylvania settled in **Kentucky** and called their settlement Harrodsburg. In 1775, Daniel Boone guided more settlers into Kentucky through the Cumberland Gap, near the Cumberland River in present-day Tennessee. The trail he blazed is called the Wilderness Road. Boone started a settlement in Kentucky near present-day Lexington and called the settlement Boonesborough.

Kentucky became part of Virginia in 1776. Many people from Virginia moved to Kentucky. After a series of British-supported Indian attacks, the settlers cut off the supply of weapons the British gave to the Indians. The settlers gained control of the land and drew up a constitution. In 1792, Kentucky became a state.

Louisiana
"The Pelican State"

Capital	State Bird
Baton Rouge	Brown pelican

State Flower	Land Area
Magnolia	43,566 sq. mi.
	(112,836 sq. km)

State Tree	Rank in Size
Bald cypress	33rd

Louisiana was once a French colony, named for King Louis XIV of France. Its first settlement was Natchitoches, founded in 1714. In 1718, New Orleans was founded. New Orleans became the capital of Louisiana in 1722.

In 1803, France sold the territory to the United States for about $15 million as part of the Louisiana Purchase, doubling what was then the United States. Louisiana included parts of Montana, North Dakota, South Dakota, Iowa, Missouri, New Mexico, Colorado, Oklahoma, Minnesota, Nebraska, Kansas, and Arkansas.

After the purchase, Congress divided the territory into smaller parts. What we now call Louisiana was known as the Territory of Orleans. In 1812, it was renamed Louisiana and became a state.

 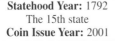

Statehood Year: 1792
The 15th state
Coin Issue Year: 2001

Statehood Year: 1812
The 18th state
Coin Issue Year: 2002

Maine
"The Pine Tree State"

Capital	State Bird
Augusta	Chickadee

State Flower	Land Area
White pine cone and tassel	30,865 sq. mi. (79,939 sq. km)

State Tree	Rank in Size
White pine	39th

Ferdinando Gorges from England came to present-day **Maine** and established the city of Gorgeana, now called York, in 1641. Other communities in the region settled by the English during that time included Kittery, Wells, Casco Bay, Kennebunk, and Scarborough. In the mid-1600s, Maine was made part of the Massachusetts Bay Colony.

During the Revolutionary War, patriots from Maine captured the British ship *Margaretta*. The British occupied the Maine community of Castine in 1779. After the war, soldiers from Maine who fought were rewarded with parcels of land.

Maine did not push for statehood until after the War of 1812. In 1819, the people of Maine voted for separation from the Massachusetts Bay Colony. One year later, Maine became the 23rd state.

 Statehood Year: 1820
The 23rd state
Coin Issue Year: 2003

Maryland
"The Old Line State"

Capital	State Bird
Annapolis	Baltimore oriole

State Flower	Land Area
Black-eyed Susan	9,775 sq. mi. (25,316 sq. km)

State Tree	Rank in Size
White oak	42nd

The first colonial settlement in what is now called **Maryland** was a trading post settled by William Claiborne on Kent Island in 1631. A year later, King Charles I of England granted the area of Maryland to Cecilius Calvert, the second Lord Baltimore. Calvert sent colonists to Maryland in 1634. They settled in St. Mary's City. In 1649, Calvert drew up a law that enforced religious tolerance, and many people came to Maryland to worship freely. The colony adopted its first constitution in 1776.

Maryland refused to become a state until colonies claiming land in the west that was not part of their official boundaries gave up that land. Their demands were met in 1781, and Maryland became the seventh state in 1788.

 Statehood Year: 1788
The 7th state
Coin Issue Year: 2000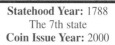

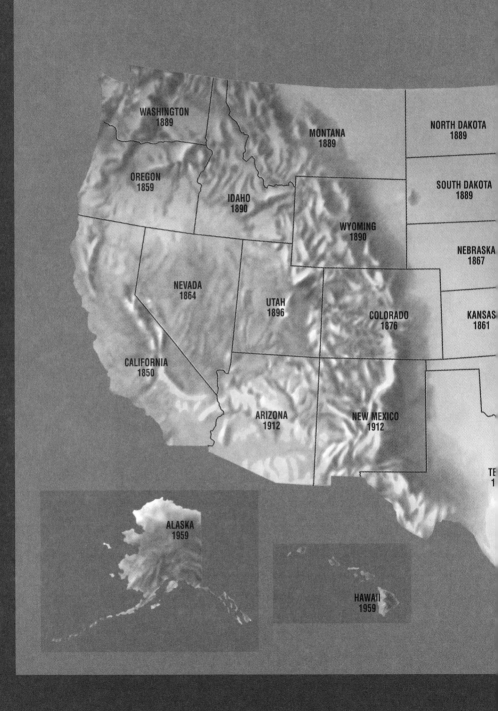

WASHINGTON
1889

MONTANA
1889

NORTH DAKOTA
1889

OREGON
1859

IDAHO
1890

SOUTH DAKOTA
1889

WYOMING
1890

NEBRASKA
1867

NEVADA
1864

UTAH
1896

COLORADO
1876

KANSAS
1861

CALIFORNIA
1850

ARIZONA
1912

NEW MEXICO
1912

TE
1

ALASKA
1959

HAWAII
1959

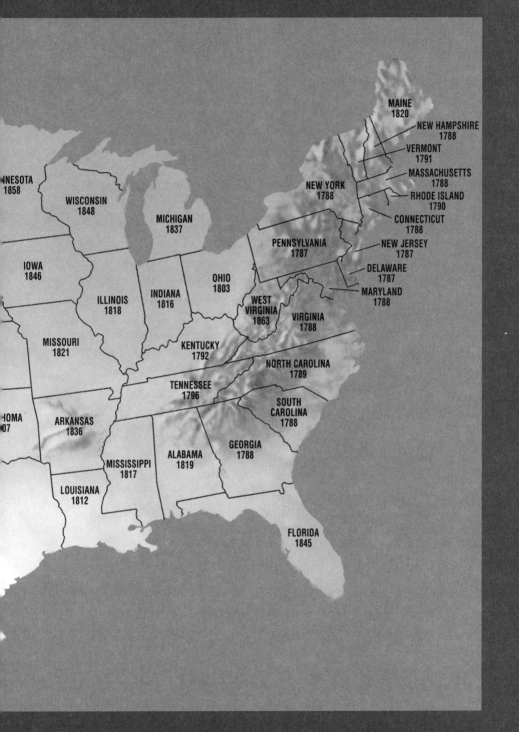

MAINE
1820

NEW HAMPSHIRE
1788

VERMONT
1791

MASSACHUSETTS
1788

RHODE ISLAND
1790

CONNECTICUT
1788

NEW JERSEY
1787

DELAWARE
1787

MARYLAND
1788

NEW YORK
1788

PENNSYLVANIA
1787

NNESOTA
1858

WISCONSIN
1848

MICHIGAN
1837

OHIO
1803

WEST
VIRGINIA
1863

VIRGINIA
1788

IOWA
1846

ILLINOIS
1818

INDIANA
1816

MISSOURI
1821

KENTUCKY
1792

NORTH CAROLINA
1789

TENNESSEE
1796

HOMA
07

ARKANSAS
1836

SOUTH
CAROLINA
1788

ALABAMA
1819

GEORGIA
1788

MISSISSIPPI
1817

LOUISIANA
1812

FLORIDA
1845

Massachusetts
"The Bay State"

Capital	**State Bird**
Boston	Chickadee
State Flower	**Land Area**
Mayflower	7,838 sq. mi.
	(20,300 sq. km)
State Tree	
American elm	**Rank in Size**
	45th

In 1620, the first Pilgrims left the Church of England to worship more freely. Their ship, the *Mayflower*, reached America in December, setting ashore in present-day **Massachusetts**. The settlers called their new colony Plymouth, after the town they sailed from in England.

In 1630, a religious group called the Puritans left England to settle the Massachusetts Bay Colony. They founded Boston that same year. In 1691, the Plymouth Colony and the Massachusetts Bay Colony combined. After England imposed several new taxes on the colonies, they began to rebel. Lexington was the site of the first shots fired in the Revolutionary War, and much of the fighting that took place during the war was in Massachusetts. In 1788, Massachusetts became a state.

Michigan
"The Wolverine State"

Capital	**State Bird**
Lansing	Robin
State Flower	**Land Area**
Apple blossom	56,809 sq. mi.
	(147,136 sq. km)
State Tree	
White pine	**Rank in Size**
	22nd

Michigan was first explored by the French, who came down from Canada. Father Rene Menard built a mission at Keweenaw Bay in 1660, and Father Jacques Marquette established the first permanent settlement in Michigan in 1668 at Sault Sainte Marie. In 1701, another French Canadian, Antoine de Lamothe Cadillac, founded Fort Pontchartrain, which became the city of Detroit.

After the French and Indian War, the French left the area and the British moved in. But in the following years, many British settlers were killed by Indians. In 1774, the British gave the land to Quebec. After the Revolutionary War, the United States gained control of Michigan. The region became part of the Northwest Territory and was admitted to statehood in 1837.

Statehood Year: 1788
The 6th state
Coin Issue Year: 2000

Statehood Year: 1837
The 26th state
Coin Issue Year: 2004

Minnesota
"The Gopher State"

Capital	**State Bird**
St. Paul	Common loon
State Flower	**Land Area**
Pink and white	79,617 sq. mi.
lady slipper	(206,207 sq. km)
State Tree	**Rank in Size**
Norway pine	14th

After the French and Indian War ended in 1763, France gave Great Britain most of its land east of the Mississippi, including eastern **Minnesota**. After the Revolutionary War, the British gave the land to the United States, but the British still hunted and trapped furs there. The United States gained the western part of present-day Minnesota in the Louisiana Purchase, but did not win complete control of the region until after the War of 1812.

In 1820, U.S. troops built Fort St. Anthony where the Mississippi and Minnesota rivers meet. Five years later, the fort was renamed Fort Snelling. The settlement became a hub for explorers, traders, and military activity. In 1849, Congress created the Minnesota Territory. At the time about 4,000 settlers were living in the territory. Minnesota became a state in 1858.

 Statehood Year: 1858
The 32nd state
Coin Issue Year: 2005

Mississippi
"The Magnolia State"

Capital	**State Bird**
Jackson	Mockingbird
State Flower	**Land Area**
Magnolia	46,914 sq. mi.
	(121,506 sq. km)
State Tree	**Rank in Size**
Magnolia	31st

Mississippi was part of French explorer La Salle's claim for France in 1682. In 1699, the first French settlement was established near present-day Ocean Springs. A second settlement was established by Jean Baptiste Le Moyne, Sieur de Bienville, who built Fort Rosalie near present-day Natchez in 1716.

Congress established the Mississippi Territory in 1798. The territory was considered valuable because ownership of it allowed access to the Mississippi River and the port of New Orleans. In the late 1700s and early 1800s, Native Americans controlled much of the Mississippi region. Mississippi became a state in 1817. By 1832, most of the Native Americans who lived there had been forced to move to Oklahoma.

 Statehood Year: 1817
The 20th state
Coin Issue Year: 2002

Missouri

"The Show Me State"

Capital	State Bird
Jefferson City	Bluebird
State Flower	**Land Area**
Hawthorn	68,898 sq. mi.
	(178,446 sq. km)
State Tree	**Rank in Size**
Flowering dogwood	18th

In 1735, settlers from Illinois set up Sainte Genevieve, **Missouri**'s first permanent community founded by Europeans. In 1762, France secretly gave Spain the region west of the Mississippi River, including Missouri. St. Louis was founded by two Frenchmen, Pierre Laclede Liguest and Rene Auguste Chouteau, in 1764.

Napoleon Bonaparte, the ruler of France, forced Spain to turn the region back over to France in 1800. Three years later, France sold the Louisiana Territory, which included present-day Missouri, to the United States. Missouri became a state in 1821. At that time it was the westernmost border of the United States.

Statehood Year: 1821
The 24th state
Coin Issue Year: 2003

Montana

"The Treasure State"

Capital	State Bird
Helena	Western meadowlark
State Flower	**Land Area**
Bitterroot	145,556 sq. mi.
	(376,991 sq. km)
State Tree	**Rank in Size**
Ponderosa pine	4th

In 1805, President Thomas Jefferson sent Meriwether Lewis and William Clark to explore **Montana** and other western regions. In 1807, fur traders began to come to Montana. Jesuit missionaries came to the region in the 1840s and established a mission near present-day Stevensville. The population of Montana grew when gold was discovered in Grasshopper Creek in 1862.

In 1876, Lieutenant Colonel George Custer's regiment and the Sioux and Cheyenne tribes fought a famous battle near the Little Bighorn River. The Indians defeated Custer's troops, killing Custer and more than 200 of his men. When the Northern Pacific Railroad came into Montana in 1883, more people came to the territory. In 1889, Montana became a state.

Statehood Year: 1889
The 41st state
Coin Issue Year: 2007

Nebraska
"The Cornhusker State"

Capital Lincoln	**State Bird** Western meadowlark
State Flower Goldenrod	**Land Area** 76,878 sq. mi. (199,113 sq. km)
State Tree Cottonwood	**Rank in Size** 15th

In the 1700s and 1800s, Indian tribes moved west to **Nebraska** after being driven from their homes by European settlers. For many years the United States kept Nebraska as Indian country and would not allow settlers to establish homes there. In 1819, the U.S. Army built Fort Atkinson, near present-day Omaha.

In 1854, Congress passed the Kansas-Nebraska Act, creating the territories of Kansas and Nebraska. By 1860, more than 28,000 people had settled in the Nebraska Territory. In 1862, Congress passed the Homestead Act. The Homestead Act gave free land to settlers in Nebraska and other western regions. As a result, thousands of people came to Nebraska. Many of the settlers became farmers. In 1867, Nebraska became a state.

Statehood Year: 1867
The 37th state
Coin Issue Year: 2006

Nevada
"The Silver State"

Capital Carson City	**State Bird** Mountain bluebird
State Flower Sagebrush	**Land Area** 109,806 sq. mi. (284,396 sq. km)
State Tree Bristlecone pine and the Single-leaf piñon	**Rank in Size** 7th

Mexico gave the United States **Nevada** and other nearby lands in 1848. In 1849, Joseph Smith and the Mormons settled in Nevada, Utah, and parts of other present-day states. Their leader, Brigham Young, called the area the State of Deseret. But Congress refused to recognize that state, and in 1850 established the Utah Territory, which included most of Nevada. Brigham Young was made the governor of the territory.

After silver was discovered in 1859, thousands of people came from the East to Nevada. They settled in a town they called Virginia City. As a result of this population growth, President Buchanan made Nevada a territory in 1861. Soon after, in 1864, President Lincoln made Nevada a state.

 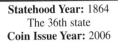

Statehood Year: 1864
The 36th state
Coin Issue Year: 2006

New Hampshire
"The Granite State"

Capital Concord	**State Bird** Purple finch
State Flower Purple lilac	**Land Area** 8,969 sq. mi (23,231 sq. km)
State Tree White birch	**Rank in Size** 44th

New Hampshire was first settled in 1623, three years after the Pilgrims landed at Plymouth Rock in Massachusetts. The English settlers landed near present-day Rye. They called their settlement Odiorne's Point. A few years later, Edward Hilton and other settlers established Hilton's Point, which is now Dover. In 1641, the Massachusetts colony took over New Hampshire. And in 1680, New Hampshire became a separate royal colony.

Several battles of the French and Indian War took place on New Hampshire soil from 1689 to 1763. In December of 1774, a group of New Hampshire colonists stole supplies from a British fort in New Castle, which helped spark the Revolutionary War. In 1776, New Hampshire created its own constitution, making it the first colony to claim its independence from Britain. The colony became a state in 1788.

 Statehood Year: 1788 The 9th state **Coin Issue Year:** 2000

New Jersey
"The Garden State"

Capital Trenton	**State Bird** Eastern goldfinch
State Flower Purple violet	**Land Area** 7,419 sq. mi. (19,215 sq. km)
State Tree Red oak	**Rank in Size** 46th

In 1660, Dutch settlers founded the permanent settlement of Bergen, which was a fortified town in present-day **New Jersey**. Bergen was New Jersey's first permanent colonial settlement and is now part of Jersey City.

In 1664, Great Britain won control of New Jersey. Before the Revolutionary War, the British began making laws that many colonists thought were unfair. One of the laws forced the colonists to pay a tax on British goods. Some residents of New Jersey protested the tax by holding a tea party similar to the more famous Boston Tea Party. They snuck on board British ships and burned boxes of tea. In 1776, New Jersey declared its independence from Britain. It became a state in 1787.

 Statehood Year: 1787 The 3rd state **Coin Issue Year:** 1999

New Mexico
"The Land of Enchantment"

Capital	**State Bird**
Santa Fe	Roadrunner
State Flower	**Land Area**
Yucca	121,365 sq. mi.
	(314,334 sq. km)
State Tree	
Piñon pine	**Rank in Size**
	5th

The Spaniards set up a colony in **New Mexico** in 1598. About 10 years later, the colony established its capital in Santa Fe, making that city the oldest seat of government in the United States. The Spaniards forced the local Indians to work for them, and the Pueblo Indians fought back in 1680. They pushed the Spaniards out of their land for a while, but in 1692, the Spaniards took over again. This time, the Spaniards and the Indians got along peacefully.

New Mexico became part of Mexico in 1821, but its residents often rebelled against Mexican rule. With the help of forces from the United States, they won independence from Mexico. The colony became a territory in 1850 and a state in 1912.

 Statehood Year: 1912
The 47th state
Coin Issue Year: 2008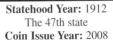

New York
"The Empire State"

Capital	**State Bird**
Albany	Bluebird
State Flower	**Land Area**
Rose	47,224 sq. mi.
	(122,310 sq. km)
State Tree	
Sugar maple	**Rank in Size**
	30th

In 1609, explorer Henry Hudson sailed up what is now called the Hudson River in **New York** looking for a water route to the Orient. Because he had been hired by the Netherlands, he claimed the region for that country. Later, it was called New Netherland. Present-day New York City was settled by the Dutch and named New Amsterdam, after the Netherlands' capital city. England took over New Netherland in 1664 and renamed it New York, after the Duke of York. But as a result of the Revolutionary War, New York won its independence from England.

New York City was the nation's capital from 1785 to 1790. George Washington took the oath of office there in 1789 to become the nation's first president. In 1788, New York became a state.

 Statehood Year: 1788
The 11th state
Coin Issue Year: 2001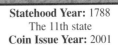

North Carolina
"The Tar Heel State"

Capital Raleigh	**State Bird** Cardinal
State Flower Flowering dogwood	**Land Area** 48,718 sq. mi. (126,180 sq. km)
State Tree Longleaf pine	**Rank in Size** 29th

In 1585, the English established a colony on Roanoke Island, just off present-day **North Carolina**. Their governor went back to England for supplies and returned in 1590 to find the colony deserted. No one knows what happened to the people who lived there.

Settlers from Virginia moved to North Carolina in 1650 and established a settlement near Albemarle Sound. The region that is now North and South Carolina was known as the Carolina colony. In 1705, a town called Bath was set up near the mouth of the Pamlico River. But settlement was difficult because the colonists had to fight Indians, and pirates sailed along the shores. In 1729, North Carolina became a royal colony, ruled by governors appointed by the king of Great Britain. North Carolina became one of the original 13 states in 1789.

Statehood Year: 1789
The 12th state
Coin Issue Year: 2001

North Dakota
"The Peace Garden State"

Capital Bismarck	**State Bird** Western meadowlark
State Flower Wild prairie rose	**Land Area** 68,994 sq. mi. (178,695 sq. km)
State Tree American elm	**Rank in Size** 17th

Lewis and Clark passed through **North Dakota** during their expedition to the Pacific Ocean. They built Fort Mandan on the Missouri River near present-day Washburn and made their winter camp there, staying until April 1805. In the 1800s, western settlement of North Dakota was slowed by the Sioux, who fought against the takeover of their land.

The Dakota Territory was established in 1861, and the territory was opened to homesteaders. In 1881, Sitting Bull, a famous Sioux leader, surrendered to the United States, assuring peace in the region. This allowed many people from the East to settle in North Dakota. In 1889, Congress divided the territory into two parts, North Dakota and South Dakota. Later that year, North Dakota became a state.

Statehood Year: 1889
The 39th state
Coin Issue Year: 2006

Ohio
"The Buckeye State"

Capital Columbus	**State Bird** Cardinal
State Flower Scarlet carnation	**Land Area** 40,953 sq. mi. (106,067 sq. km)
State Tree Buckeye	**Rank in Size** 35th

In 1747, businessmen from Virginia and England formed the **Ohio** Company of Virginia, with plans to settle the Ohio region. The company sent explorers to the area but did not immediately establish a settlement. Ohio became part of the Northwest Territory in 1787. In 1788, the company established the first permanent territorial settlement in Ohio, called Marietta. That same year Marietta became the first capital of the Northwest Territory.

Several Indian tribes fought against the settlers who came to the territory. In 1795, peace was achieved through the Treaty of Greenville, signed by settlers and Indian leaders. The Indians gave two-thirds of the Ohio region to the United States. After this treaty was signed, many more settlers came to Ohio. In 1803, Ohio became a state.

Statehood Year: 1803
The 17th state
Coin Issue Year: 2002

Oklahoma
"The Sooner State"

Capital Oklahoma City	**State Bird** Scissor-tailed flycatcher
State Flower Mistletoe	**Land Area** 68,679 sq. mi. (177,877 sq. km)
State Tree Redbud	**Rank in Size** 19th

For hundreds of years, Cheyenne, Comanche, Pawnee, Wichita, and other Native American tribes roamed the plains and hunted for buffalo on the sprawling grasslands in present-day **Oklahoma**. But in the 1800s, the United States government bought up their land and forced them onto reservations. Then the government began moving tribes from other parts of the country to Oakahoma. But on April 22, 1889, central Oklahoma was opened for settlement to people other than Indians. About 50,000 people had moved in by evening.

In 1890, the United States created the Territory of Oklahoma. Maps of that time outline divisions in the territory between Indian Territory and Oklahoma Territory. In 1893, with encouragement from Congress, the Indian nations dissolved, and the tribes incorporated towns and became U.S. citizens. In 1907, Oklahoma became a state.

Statehood Year: 1907
The 46th state
Coin Issue Year: 2008

Oregon
"The Beaver State"

Capital
Salem

State Bird
Western meadowlark

State Flower
Oregon grape

Land Area
96,003 sq. mi.
(248,646 sq. km)

State Tree
Douglas fir

Rank in Size
10th

British and American explorers had sailed into the Columbia River, on the northern border of **Oregon,** in the late 1800s. But Lewis and Clark were the first to travel down the river from the east during their famous expedition.

Fur trading was important in the early development of Oregon. In 1811, John Jacob Astor formed the first European settlement, Astoria, at the mouth of the Columbia River. A British trading company took over Astoria in 1813. In the 1800s, many American and British fur trading companies opened in Oregon. John McLoughlin, the British director of the Hudson's Bay Company, ruled the region for about 20 years and helped many people settle there. He is known as the father of Oregon. In 1848, Oregon became a territory. The territory achieved statehood in 1859.

Statehood Year: 1859
The 33rd state
Coin Issue Year: 2005

Pennsylvania
"The Keystone State"

Capital
Harrisburg

State Bird
Ruffed grouse

State Flower
Mountain laurel

Land Area
44,820 sq.mi.
(116,083 sq. km)

State Tree
Hemlock

Rank in Size
32nd

Pennsylvania was settled by Swedish and Dutch immigrants in the mid-1600s. In 1664, the English captured the region. They gave the land to William Penn in 1681 as payment for a debt owed to Penn's father. Penn came to Pennsylvania (which means "Penn's Woods") in 1682 with fellow Quakers and governed the land. His family governed Pennsylvania until the start of the Revolutionary War in 1775.

The city of Philadelphia was the nation's capital from 1790 to 1800. It was here that the Continental Congress adopted the Declaration of Independence in 1776 and the Constitutional Convention adopted the United States Constitution in 1787. In 1787, Pennsylvania was the second state admitted into the Union.

Statehood Year: 1787
The 2nd state
Coin Issue Year: 1999

Rhode Island
"The Ocean State"

Capital Providence	**State Bird** Rhode Island Red
State Flower Violet	**Land Area** 1,045 sq. mi. (2,707 sq. km)
State Tree Red maple	**Rank in Size** 50th

Roger Williams established the first English settlement in **Rhode Island** in 1636. He founded the community of Providence on land he bought from two Narragansett Indian chiefs. He was followed by others looking for religious freedom. Rhode Island was a prosperous region. Its location on the ocean made its city of Newport a busy port.

In 1774, Rhode Island became the first colony to stop the importation of slaves by prohibiting slave trade. Rhode Islanders were also among the first to rebel against British authority. In 1769, they burned the British ship *Liberty*, which was docked at Newport. Another first occurred on May 4, 1776, when Rhode Island became the first of the 13 original colonies to declare its independence from Britain. Rhode Island became a state in 1790.

South Carolina
"The Palmetto State"

Capital Columbia	**State Bird** Carolina wren
State Flower Carolina jessamine	**Land Area** 30,111 sq. mi. (77,988 sq. km)
State Tree Palmetto	**Rank in Size** 40th

South Carolina was settled as a British colony in 1670, but the king allowed the settlers to rule themselves because he considered the South Carolina coast important in the colony's defense against invaders. The colonists established a settlement at Albemarle Point, near present-day Charleston. In 1680, they moved to Oyster Point and called their settlement Charles Town. Later the spelling was changed to Charleston.

In the early 1700s, the settlers fought off French and Spanish forces and attacks from Indians and pirates. The colonists soon rebelled against their British proprietors, who did nothing to help them fight off these invaders. In 1710, the colony was divided into North and South Carolina. In 1788, South Carolina became a state.

Statehood Year: 1790
The 13th state
Coin Issue Year: 2001

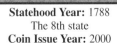

Statehood Year: 1788
The 8th state
Coin Issue Year: 2000

South Dakota
"The Mount Rushmore State"

Capital	**State Bird**
Pierre	Ring-necked pheasant
State Flower	**Land Area**
Pasque	75,896 sq. mi.
	(196,571 sq. km)
State Tree	**Rank in Size**
Black Hills spruce	16th

In 1817, a French fur trader named Joseph La Framboise built the first permanent European settlement in **South Dakota**, a trading post at present-day Fort Pierre. The area was opened up to active trading when a steamboat traveled up the Missouri River. In 1857, land companies began developing towns along the Missouri River. Congress officially created the Dakota Territory in 1861, which included present-day South Dakota and North Dakota.

In 1874, Lieutenant Colonel George Custer and his men found gold in the Black Hills, and a gold rush began. More gold was found in 1876, and more prospectors rushed to join the search. As the region's population grew, its residents pushed for statehood. In 1889, South Dakota became a state.

 Statehood Year: 1889
The 40th state
Coin Issue Year: 2006

Tennessee
"The Volunteer State"

Capital	**State Bird**
Nashville	Mockingbird
State Flower	**Land Area**
Iris	41,220 sq. mi.
	(106,759 sq. km)
State Tree	**Rank in Size**
Tulip poplar	34th

In 1714, a French fur trader established a trading post near present-day Nashville, **Tennessee**. By the 1760s, there were many settlers in Tennessee, which was then part of North Carolina. But the mountains separated them from the eastern colonies. In 1775, the Transylvania Company, which had just bought a huge piece of land from the Cherokee Indians, hired Daniel Boone to blaze a trail near the corner where Virginia, Kentucky, and Tennessee meet at a pass in the mountains called the Cumberland Gap. The trail became known as the Wilderness Road. Its construction allowed more people to settle in Tennessee. In 1796, Tennessee became a state, although the Chickasaw and Cherokee tribes still occupied much of the region. In 1818, the Chickasaw sold most of the land to the U.S. government. The Chickasaw remained, but were later forced to leave.

 Statehood Year: 1796
The 16th state
Coin Issue Year: 2002

Texas
"The Lone Star State"

Capital	**State Bird**
Austin	Mockingbird
State Flower	**Land Area**
Bluebonnet	261,914 sq. mi.
	(678,358 sq. km)
State Tree	**Rank in Size**
Pecan	2nd

Texas was once a part of Mexico. But many Texans wanted their freedom, so they started the Texas Revolution in 1835. The most famous battle between Texas and Mexico took place in 1836 at the Alamo, a Spanish mission in San Antonio. There, 189 Texans fought thousands of Mexican soldiers. The fighting lasted 13 days, but the Mexican Army eventually won, led by General Santa Anna. The famous frontiersmen Davy Crockett and Jim Bowie fought and died at the Alamo. Led by General Sam Houston, Texas fought back about a month later and gained its independence from Mexico.

After becoming a state in 1845, Texas left the Union in 1861 to join the Confederacy. The state was readmitted to the Union in 1870.

Utah
"The Beehive State"

Capital	**State Bird**
Salt Lake City	Seagull
State Flower	**Land Area**
Sego lily	82,168 sq. mi.
	(212,816 sq. km)
State Tree	**Rank in Size**
Blue spruce	12th

In 1847, the Mormons, a religious group led by Brigham Young, arrived in **Utah** and started the area's first major settlement. For several years the region was almost exclusively Mormon. In 1850, Congress created the Utah Territory, with Brigham Young as its governor. Many people in Utah wanted statehood, but Congress was concerned that the Mormon church was too involved in the area's government and did not agree with the Mormon practice of polygamy (when a man marries more than one wife). But in 1890, the Mormon church president advised Mormons to give up polygamy. Not long after that, the Mormon church agreed to lessen its control on the territory, and Utah became a state in 1896.

 Statehood Year: 1845
The 28th state
Coin Issue Year: 2004

 Statehood Year: 1896
The 45th state
Coin Issue Year: 2007

Vermont
"The Green Mountain State"

Capital	**State Bird**
Montpelier	Hermit thrush
State Flower	**Land Area**
Red clover	9,249 sq. mi.
	(23,956 sq. km)
State Tree	**Rank in Size**
Sugar maple	43rd

In 1770, the "Green Mountain Boys," a military force made up of men from **Vermont**, banded together to drive out settlers from New York who had laid claim to some of the land in Vermont. At the time, Vermont was called "New Hampshire Grants." The Green Mountain Boys also fought and won some important battles in the Revolutionary War, including the capture of the Brtish Fort Ticonderoga in 1775. That victory was one of the most critical in the early stages of the war.

In 1777, Vermont declared that it was an independent republic, called New Connecticut. In July of that year, the republic adopted a constitution and changed its name to Vermont, from the French for "green mountain." It remained an independent republic until 1791, when it became a state.

Statehood Year: 1791
The 14th state
Coin Issue Year: 2001

Virginia
"Old Dominion"

Capital	**State Bird**
Richmond	Cardinal
State Flower	**Land Area**
American dogwood	39,598 sq. mi.
	(102,558 sq. km)
State Tree	**Rank in Size**
American dogwood	37th

The first permanent English settlement in the colonies was in **Virginia**'s Jamestown, settled in 1607. In 1619, it was the site of the meeting of America's first legislative assembly. But the settlement suffered many setbacks. In 1622, Indians attacked Jamestown and killed hundreds of its residents. With Jamestown as its capital, Virginia became a royal colony in 1624, governed by leaders sent from England. The capital was moved from Jamestown to Williamsburg in 1699, then to Richmond in 1780.

In 1788, Virginia became a state. One year later, George Washington, a Virginian, was elected as the first President of the United States. Three of the next four Presidents were also from Virginia.

Statehood Year: 1788
The 10th state
Coin Issue Year: 2000

Washington
"The Evergreen State"

Capital	State Bird
Olympia	Willow goldfinch

State Flower
Coast rhododendron

Land Area
66,581 sq. mi.
(172,445 sq. km)

State Tree
Western hemlock

Rank in Size
20th

Washington was settled by British and American traders. In 1818, the two countries signed a treaty that allowed them to trade and settle in the region, which was called the Oregon Country at the time. But even after the treaty, the countries could not agree on the boundary. In 1846, the two countries came to an agreement, and President Polk signed another treaty with Great Britain. What is now the state of Washington went to America, while the British kept Vancouver Island.

The Oregon Territory was founded in 1848 and included Washington. Five years later, Washington became a separate territory with its capital at Olympia. In 1883, railroad lines were completed that linked Washington with the Eastern United States. Washington became a state in 1889.

West Virginia
"The Mountain State"

Capital	State Bird
Charleston	Cardinal

State Flower
Rhododendron

Land Area
24,087 sq. mi.
(62,384 sq. km)

State Tree
Sugar maple

Rank in Size
41st

West Virginia was once part of the Virginia Colony, granted to a group of English merchants and investors in 1606. Early on, the western part of the colony demanded its own government. Farmers in the west did not appreciate being ruled by aristocrats in eastern Virginia. In the mid-1800s, the region became even more divided over the slavery debate. Eastern Virginia had many large plantations with hundreds of slaves. The plantation owners controlled the government, and the westerners felt they were not fairly represented.

When the Civil War began in 1861, the western region declared its independence from Virginia and joined the side of the Union states. West Virginia became a state in 1863.

 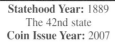

Statehood Year: 1889
The 42nd state
Coin Issue Year: 2007

Statehood Year: 1863
The 35th state
Coin Issue Year: 2005

Wisconsin
"The Badger State"

Capital
Madison

State Bird
Robin

State Flower
Wood violet

Land Area
54,314 sq. mi.
(140,672 sq. km)

State Tree
Sugar maple

Rank in Size
25th

The first European to see **Wisconsin** was Frenchman Jean Nicolet. Searching for a water route to China, he sailed from Quebec to what is now called Green Bay. When he landed on the shore in 1634, he expected to be greeted by Chinese officials. Instead, he met Winnebago Indians. Disappointed, Nicolet returned to Quebec and told people there that America was even larger than they thought.

French missionary Father Rene Menard established a mission near present-day Ashland in 1660. Other missionaries followed and set up more missions. In 1774, Wisconsin was made part of Quebec.

Wisconsin became a territory of the United States in 1836 and achieved statehood in 1848.

 Statehood Year: 1848
The 30th state
Coin Issue Year: 2004

Wyoming
"The Equality State"

Capital
Cheyenne

State Bird
Meadowlark

State Flower
Indian paintbrush

Land Area
97,105 sq. mi.
(251,501 sq. km)

State Tree
Cottonwood

Rank in Size
9th

In the 1800s, three important trails went through **Wyoming**: the California Trail, the Mormon Trail, and the Oregon Trail. Pioneers from the East followed these trails through the South Pass, which wound through the Rocky Mountains.

In 1846, Congress voted to build forts along the Oregon Trail to protect pioneers from Indian attacks. The first American trading post, Fort William, had been set up in 1834 by two trappers in eastern Wyoming. The United States government later bought Fort William and renamed it Fort Laramie.

The Territory of Wyoming was organized in 1868. In 1874, gold was discovered in the Black Hills, and prospectors rushed to the region. Wyoming became a state in 1890.

 Statehood Year: 1890
The 44th state
Coin Issue Year: 2007